Our Family's Christmas Elf

Carol Sbordon Bannon
In collaboration with
Edna Jean Sbordon Halbach

AuthorHouse™
1663 Liberty Drive, Suite 200
Bloomington, IN 47403
www.authorhouse.com
Phone: 1-800-839-8640

AuthorHouse™ UK Ltd.
500 Avebury Boulevard
Central Milton Keynes, MK9 2BE
www.authorhouse.co.uk
Phone: 08001974150

First published by AuthorHouse 9/29/2006

ISBN: 1-4259-4310-1 (sc)

Printed in the United States of America
Bloomington, Indiana

This book is printed on acid-free paper.

"Illustrations by Joe Lee"

Bloomington, IN Milton Keynes, UK

authorHOUSE

<u>Acknowledgments</u>

This story could not have happened without my brother and sister. Bill never let us forget our own childhood elves, and it is because of his Christmas spirit the elves still manage to find their way into all of our homes some 45 years later.

Edna Jean is not only my sister and collaborator; she is my best friend. She has been instrumental and supportive through all of the many rewrites.

We also need to thank our husbands, Cliff and Hank, for their encouragement, patience, and support.

*This book is dedicated to William and Edna Sbordon,
and their 14 grandchildren*

One week before Christmas and everyone is busy.
It is hard to sit still, and even harder to be good.

Then, on December 17th, he comes.

Do you see him?
Can you find him?
Be careful you don't scare him.

There he is, hiding behind the apples....
Our family's Christmas elf!

He smells the cookies. He watches us decorate.
He shares in the fun, and isn't any trouble!

The next morning, he is ---

Oh no! He is not on the table.

Do you see him?
Can you find him?
Be careful you don't scare him.

There he is, hiding on the mantle behind the candles and the ribbons. He is enjoying the fire and he looks happy.

Our elf watches as we decorate the Christmas tree.

It is very pretty.

It is December 19th and we have snow.

Everyone is home. Dad has turned on our Christmas tree lights, but our elf is gone.

Do you see him?
Can you find him?
Be careful you don't scare him.

He is hiding inside the Christmas tree, next to Mom's favorite ornament. He can see himself.

It is getting closer and closer to Christmas Eve. We wonder if our elf misses the North Pole and Santa.

Today is December 20th and we are going shopping.

Our elf will have to stay by himself. OH NO! He is gone *again*.

Do you see him?
Can you find him?
Be careful you don't scare him.

There he is, sitting on the front door ledge.
He laughs as we scramble for our hats and mittens.
Mom says to slow down. Dad says to hurry up.

When we come home our elf will see everything we bought.

It is December 21ˢᵗ. We still need to finish decorating.

OH NO! He's not on the front door ledge.

Do you see him?
Can you find him?
Be careful you don't scare him.

Oh my! Isn't he a silly elf? He is on the foyer light, hanging upside down.

We wonder what he's looking at.

Today is December 22nd and we are going to wrap presents.

Our elf can watch us from the foyer light.
OH NO! Where has he gone *now?*

Do you see him?
Can you find him?
Be careful you don't scare him.

Look at our Christmas elf.
He is hiding on the refrigerator by our cookies.

We always have enough cookies and treats for family and friends. We even make special ones for Santa.

It is the day before Santa comes...December 23rd!

OH NO! Our elf is not on the refrigerator.
Did he fall into the freezer? Did we give him away in a gift bag?

Do you see him?
Can you find him?
Be careful you don't scare him.

We see him. He's sitting in the middle of Mom's wreath. He found the perfect place. He watches as we place special gifts under the tree.

Only 1 more day.

It is Christmas Eve. Tonight Santa comes. Our elf will see him come down the chimney.

OH NO! He is not on the wreath.
We must find him.

Do you see him?
Can you find him?
Be careful you don't scare him.

Look! He is sitting by the manger, reminding us that tonight is a holy night, a special night.

Soon we will put on our pajamas and hurry to bed.

Goodnight, Christmas elf.

It is Christmas morning.

Santa has come. I am sure our elf told him we were
very good.

Look at our tree.   Look at all the presents.
And sitting right on top of everything is ----

Our family's Christmas elf.

He enjoys watching as we open and play with our new presents. We are very careful not to lose him in all the wrappings.

Our elf loves Christmas as much as we do.

And the next day, when Christmas Day is over, our family's Christmas elf is----

Gone!

Do you see him?

Can you find him?

You don't have to worry. You will not scare him.

Our elf has gone home to the North Pole.
But next year he will come again.

We will just have to wait.

About the Author

Carol S. Bannon is a full time writer with a degree in elementary education. Her experience teaching children with reading difficulties was instrumental in the writing of <u>Our Family's Christmas Elf</u>. Although she has always enjoyed writing, it was not until her family moved five years ago that she was able to indulge her desire to write full time.

She is happily married with four grown children and currently resides in Chaska, Minnesota. In addition to storytelling, she continues to tutor children with learning difficulties and substitute teaches.

Printed in the United States
63502LVS00001B